BE THE BEST ME

WRITTEN BY - THAT ONE GUY

ILLUSTRATED BY - SATHOMI EKANAYAKE

BLUE MARTIAN BOOKS
PHOENIX

Today I got up
I got right out of bed,
But something was wrong
Up inside of my head

I didn't feel good
I didn't feel right,
But what could be wrong?
I'd slept through the night

I didn't have nightmares
At least I don't think
I'd climbed Mount Olympus
I was done in a wink

I'd dreamt I ate dinner
With a fierce dinosaur
He ate a whole pizza,
But I ate even more

But the helmet wouldn't
Slide down over my face

My suit was too small
Or I was too large...
It was then that I realized
I'm as large as a barge

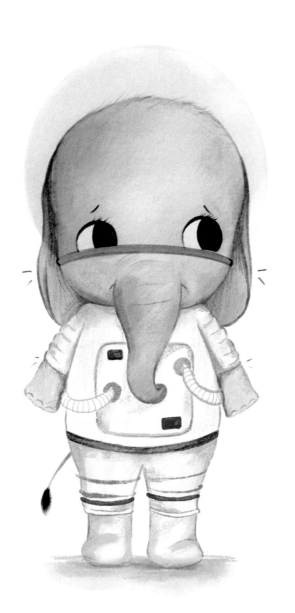

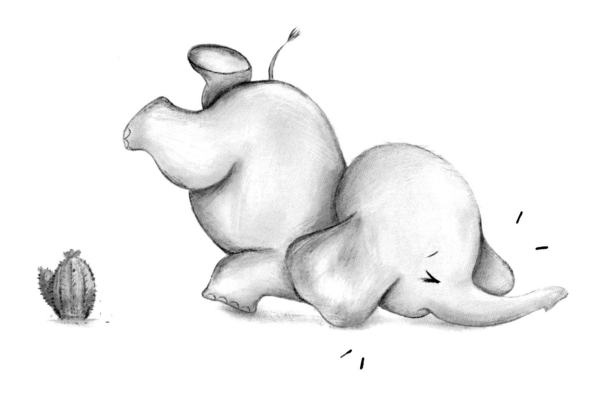

My feet are quite clumsy
My nose is colossal
And my body's as big
As a dinosaur fossil

My tail is just tiny
My skin is plain gray
And gray is the mood
Of a sad, rainy day

And that's when it happened
That's when I decided
To be something else
Oh, I was delighted!

I'd be something else
That's just what I'd do
I'd become someone new,
But who, but who?

Then I had an idea
It hit me like lightning
I'd paint my whole body
Now this was enlightening!

So then I got busy
It took a great while
I used tons of paint
To create my new style

At last I was done
I was finally free
From that boring old
Gray old gargantuous me

In the tops of the trees
I sat by a nest,
But the toucans just stared
As if I was a pest

"Hello there" I said,
"What a lov-er-ly day."
But then they all turned
And they flew far away

"No worries" I said,
"There are plenty of creatures.
I just need
To adjust my new features."

So adjust them I did
It was worth it because
My new look was sure
To create a huge buzz

Then I bizzed and I buzzed
In a field of bright flowers
Working so hard
For what felt like ten hours

Then I took a quick break
I was looking around
And my heart nearly stopped
At what my eyes found

The flowers were not
Looking happy and free
They'd smashed and they'd smooshed
And they'd squooshed beneath me

So as a small bee
I didn't quite fit,
But my next try was sure
To be a big hit

With paint once again
I made a disguise,
But this time I chose
To be something my size

To the tall trees I went
To play and to eat,
But I wasn't tall enough
Even up on two feet

I felt so ashamed,
So silly, so sour
That I bolted from there
At 100 miles per hour

Nothing felt quite right,
But what could be done?
I needed something else
Like more joy or more fun!

So to the monkeys I went
And they were friendly and kind
At last I could stay
And leave the old me behind

They urged me to play
While they were swinging around,
But the branch I chose broke
And I fell straight to the ground

"Well this won't work"
I said in my head.
"If I try swinging again
I just might end up dead."

So to the river I ran
And jumped in with a smile
Then I started to swim
With a Nile crocodile!

The water felt nice
'Til something touched me beneath
I thought "It's a fish"
Until I saw the HUGE TEETH!

I raced out in a flash
And laid in the shade
Then I had an idea
For a disguise to be made

I got right to work
It's not hard to explain
I glued leaves together
To create a lion mane

So now I'm with the lions,
But it's scarier than before
Especially when the biggest cat
Lets out a mighty ROAR!

I run away so fast
I don't even look back
That lion was so fierce
I nearly had a heart attack!

But now what do I do?
I have nowhere I can go
I don't belong anywhere
And I'm at an all-time low

Then the ground around me rumbles
A giant creature's on the move
It's feet are big and it's nose is huge
This thing is just my groove!

I watch it in amazement,
But I can't see where it went
Then I get a real good view...

IT'S ANOTHER ELEPHANT!

Right then and there
It hits me
Who I was
Born to be

Some things I can't
And shouldn't change

SO I'LL
BE THE BEST ME
I CAN POSSIBLY BE!

✓ If you loved this book, please leave a 5-star review on Amazon - thanks, this really helps us out!

✓ That One Guy Books are on ▶ YouTube!

✓ Check out That One Guy Books on Instagram for updates & tips for writing picture books

✓ Join the newsletter so you never miss an update or new book that you can trust for your child
www.thatoneguybooks.com

To my lovely, sweet wife Emily for always
encouraging me to be my best self.
                                    –That One Guy

About the Author

That One Guy has loved children's books ever since
being exposed to the lyrical rhymes and nonsensical
worlds of Dr. Seuss as a boy. He's excited to bring
smiles and laughter to kids everywhere through funny,
wholesome stories that parents can trust.
When he's not writing, he can be found braving the
Phoenix heat with his beautiful wife and three
rambunctious boys. That One Guy can be found on
YouTube, Instagram, or at
www.thatoneguybooks.com

To my niece, Emilia Kai, because of whom I
began to work on children's book illustration.
                                    –Sathomi

About the Illustrator

Sathomi Ekanayake is a Sri Lankan illustrator based in
Kyoto, Japan. She primarily works on fashion
illustration and children's book illustration. Sathomi
grew up reading her sister's picture books, and has
always loved to draw and paint. She graduated from
the Northumbria University, UK with a Bachelor of Arts
Honors in Fashion and Textile Design. During her
fashion school years, she was always passionate about
illustration more than she was in designing and
manufacturing garments. After graduating from Fashion
School in 2019, Sathomi decided to become a full-time
illustrator. At the latter part of 2020 she began her
career as a freelance illustrator and has loved it ever
since.
Instagram - @sathomi.illustrates
email- studiofour.jp@gmail.com

More Books by That One Guy

The Boring Stuff

First paperback edition August 2022

Illustrations by Sathomi Ekanayake

ISBN 978-1-958935-03-3 (paperback)
ISBN 978-1-958935-05-7 (hardcover)
ISBN 978-1-958935-04-0 (ebook)

Published by Blue Martian Books
www.thatoneguybooks.com

Made in the USA
Monee, IL
25 November 2022

18499226R00026